Windmill

Granny
Rabbit's cottage

The squirrels
lived in these woods

Mr Mole:
Tradesmen's
entrance

This is the hill
they whizzed
down

They gathered
flowers here

Frankie
Frog's house

Mr Mole's
house

da
ldmouse's
tage

Hedgehog's
house

Tasseltip takes a ride

Story by Sarah Cotton

Illustrations by
Ernest A. Aris and Roy Smith

*Based on the original characters
created by Dorothy Richards*

Publishers: Ladybird Books Ltd . Loughborough
© Ladybird Books Ltd 1975   *Printed in England*

TASSELTIP TAKES A RIDE

Mrs Rabbit added a bottle of milk to the basket of groceries on the table.

"I wonder what else I can find to send to Granny," she said to herself, and went to look in the larder.

Tasseltip finished his second helping of porridge, and decided not to ask for another, as he was in a hurry to go outside and play. It had been snowing all through the night and now everything was covered in a thick white blanket.

"It looks so lovely outside, can I go out now? I can't wait to build something in all that snow," he said.

"Before you go out to play," said Mrs Rabbit, "I want you to take this basket to Granny. She hasn't been feeling very well, and I don't want her to have to go out in this weather."

"Oh!" said Tasseltip in dismay. "Can't I go later? It's so lovely outside, I don't want to miss it."

"I think you will find the snow will last for a few more days," laughed Mrs Rabbit. "Now go and get ready to go out, and I will finish collecting things for Granny."

5

Tasseltip went to the sink and wiped his face and paws. Then he put on his warm scarf.

"Now, I want you to go straight to Granny's house," said Mrs Rabbit, using a white cloth to cover the top of the basket. "When you have made sure that she is all right, come home and tell me. Then you can go and play."

"Yes, I will," said Tasseltip, picking up the basket. "Goodbye." He opened the door and went out.

"This is fun," thought Tasseltip, going along the pathway that led to Granny's cottage. "There's so much snow I can't even see the windmill."

He put the basket down, and picked up a large handful of snow. He made it into a ball and threw it at the trunk of a tree, where it left a white mark.

Then he remembered what his mother had told him: no dawdling on his way to see Granny. He picked up the basket and set off up the hill.

Slipping and sliding along, he suddenly heard a 'swish, swish, swish' sound in the stillness.

"That's funny, I wonder what's making that peculiar noise?" thought Tasseltip. "I'd better go on, though." So, without bothering to go and see what it was, he went on his way.

"Tasseltip! Wait for me," cried Robert Rat.

"What have you got there?" Tasseltip asked his friend, looking to see what Robert was pulling behind him.

"It's only a tray," said Robert. "My mother said I could borrow it to play with."

"Why do you want a tray to play with?" asked Tasseltip, puzzled.

"To ride on, of course!" said Robert happily. "When I woke up this morning and saw all the snow, I thought it would be fun to go up to the top of the hill and ride down it on a tray."

"What a wonderful idea!" exclaimed Tasseltip, clapping his paws together. "May I play with you?"

"Of course, that's why I shouted to you to stop. I went to your house earlier this morning, but you had already gone out," said Robert.

"So it was *you* who was making that funny swishy sound I heard earlier?" Tasseltip asked.

"It does make a nice noise," said Robert. "I think it's almost as good as a real toboggan, or at least I hope it will be. I was thinking it might be fun to find a few more friends to play with us."

"Good idea," said Tasseltip, and off they went.

"Anyway, who are you going to see?" asked Robert. "And what's in that enormous basket?"

"I'm going to see Granny, she's not feeling very well," said Tasseltip. "My mother said that Granny shouldn't go out in this cold weather, so I've got some groceries and things for her."

"I'll take one side and you take the other," offered Robert, and together they walked up the hill, kicking at the snow as they went.

"Doesn't it look lovely?" said Tasseltip, when they stopped to rest a few minutes later. "Everywhere you can see is white, even the trees have bits of snow on them."

"Did you see it when it was actually snowing?" asked Robert. "I woke up when it was quite dark, and looked out of the window. It was like birds' feathers falling from the sky, all soft and very quiet."

"I wish I had seen it," said Tasseltip, a bit enviously. "I was fast asleep until it was time to get up. It was very cold though. There was a Jack Frost pattern on my window, just like feathers and ferns."

They both laughed and, picking up the basket, set off again up the hill, with Robert's tray slithering through the snow behind them. They stopped before they reached the top to have a snowball fight. They threw snow at each other and ducked and dodged, slipping and falling until they were covered in snow.

"I'd better go on," said Tasseltip, rather reluctantly, for he was thoroughly enjoying himself. "I did promise I would go straight to the cottage."

"All right," agreed Robert. "No more games until you have seen your grandmother."

"There it is," puffed Tasseltip, pointing to a small thatched cottage.

"I'll wait outside for a few minutes, just in case you aren't very long," said Robert.

Tasseltip went up to the front door, knocked, and went inside. Granny was sitting in her favourite green armchair, huddled over a small fire.

"I've brought you this," said Tasseltip, putting the basket on the table. "It's groceries and things from Mummy. It's lovely outside, all white and snowy. But it's probably better for you to stay in if you are not feeling very well."

"I think it's only a cold," said Granny, smiling.

"Robert's got a tray," Tasseltip told his Granny. "We're going to use it like a toboggan."

"Dear, dear," said Granny, shaking her head. "I think I'm too old for playing games like that. Where is young Robert?" she asked.

"He's waiting outside," Tasseltip told her.

"Goodness me! Bring him in at once," said Granny. "He'll catch a worse cold than mine!"

Tasseltip opened the door and shouted to Robert to come in.

"Good morning, Mrs Rabbit," said Robert. "Thank you for inviting me in. It's jolly cold outside if you are not doing anything."

"Of course it is," said Granny, getting up from her chair. "Now come and stand here by the fire. You'll be warm in no time. Tasseltip, dear, there *is* one thing I would like you to do for me. I need some more wood. You'll find it in the shed."

"Yes, Granny, of course," said Tasseltip. He went outside and came back in no time at all with his arms full of wood.

"That's a wonderful lot," smiled Granny, and in minutes she had the fire roaring, while Robert filled the woodbox. Then Granny started to sneeze.

"I'm lovely and warm now," Robert said to her. "I think perhaps you ought to sit down again." He pulled the armchair nearer the fire as he spoke.

"I've put everything away in the kitchen," said Tasseltip, coming back into the room carefully carrying a large cup of steaming nettle tea.

"Thank you both so much," said Granny, as she sat down and held out her paw to take the cup.

"Oh dear," said poor Granny, starting to sneeze again. "I really don't feel very well. Tasseltip, would you be a dear and go and ask kind Nurse Mole to look in and see me?"

"Of course I will," said Tasseltip. "Come on, Robert, let's go now."

"Don't forget to thank your mother for all the groceries," said Granny. "And thank you for being so helpful, both of you."

Robert collected his tray as they set off towards Mr Mole's house.

"I say, look out!" yelled Tasseltip. "Quick, duck!" But it was too late. A large snowball came flying through the air and caught Robert on the side of his head.

"What . . . who did that?" spluttered Robert, then to his amazement he saw a grinning Frankie Frog standing in front of him.

"Ha, ha," laughed Frankie. "You were a splendid target. I've been following you both for quite a while."

"Have you indeed!" said Robert grimly, and, within moments, the two were rolling in the snow wrestling each other.

"That's enough, you two," said Tasseltip, pulling them apart. "Stop fighting and be friends. It's silly to waste time when we can play in all this snow."

"You're right," said Robert, brushing the snow from his clothes. He held out his paw to Frankie, who took it and solemnly shook it.

"What are you doing up here, anyway?" asked Tasseltip curiously, when they set off again through the snow.

"My father made me help him mend two burst pipes earlier on this morning," said Frankie. "It was ages before he said I could come out to play. I went round to both your houses, but you'd gone."

"My mother made me promise to go and see my grandmother first, she's got a bad cold," said Tasseltip. "In fact, we are on our way to fetch Nurse Mole."

"I'll come with you," said Frankie, and the three walked along together.

"Hey! What's happening?" said Robert a moment later, turning round to see a laughing Susie Squirrel sitting firmly on top of his tray.

"Friskie and I have been following you through the trees," explained Susie, still laughing.

"What's going on?" said Friskie, climbing down the tree. "What are you going to do with that tray?"

"It's mine, if Susie will kindly get off it," said Robert. "I am going to use it as a toboggan. You may join us if you want to."

"Get up, Susie," said Friskie, prodding her with his foot. "Thanks Robert, we'd love to join you. Isn't the snow great? Did you see it come down last night?"

"Yes, I did," said Robert proudly, struggling to pull the tray across a particularly deep patch of snow. "It was so exciting, just like hundreds of feathers falling from the sky."

The others looked at him rather enviously because they had all been fast asleep, snug and warm.

"I was thinking of going to the hill above the meadow," Robert told Tasseltip. "If you go to Mr Mole's back door, it would save you a lot of time."

"Why are you going to see Mr Mole?" asked Susie Squirrel.

"My grandmother isn't very well, and she wants to see Nurse Mole," explained Tasseltip. "I promised to go and ask her to call."

"We'll be on the hill, then," said Robert. "Don't be too long, or you will miss all the fun."

"I shall be as quick as I can," said Tasseltip. "See you later." And off he hurried through the deep snow. It took much longer than he expected to reach Mr Mole's house, because he kept falling into deep drifts, and each time it took him several minutes before he could scramble out.

When he reached Mr Mole's back door, which had *Tradesmen's Entrance* written in big letters on it, he knocked loudly, and opened it.

Mr Mole hadn't lived in this particular house for very long and everything was nicely painted and bright. The long passageway was lit by little lanterns that hung from the ceiling and there was a mat of woven leaves and grasses along the floor. It was much warmer than outside. and Tasseltip hurried along until he reached the proper front door of Mr Mole's house. He knocked loudly again.

MR. MOLE

TRADESMEN'S ENTRANCE

"Good morning, Mr Mole," said Tasseltip politely, as the door opened.

"Why Tasseltip! What can I do for you?" said Mr Mole.

"It's my grandmother," explained Tasseltip. "She's got a terrible cold and isn't feeling well, so she asked me to see if Nurse Mole would come."

"I am so sorry to hear she isn't well," said kind Mr Mole, "but I'm afraid my sister went out to see one of Dr Badger's patients only five minutes ago. I don't think she will be very long, so I suggest you wait here. Unless you are in a great hurry?"

"Well, no," said Tasseltip, not very truthfully. Then he decided to explain. "Robert Rat has got an old tray from his mother, and he and the Squirrels and Frankie Frog are playing with it. They are using it as a toboggan. I'm going to play with it, too, after I have seen your sister."

Mr Mole laughed. "I expect walking in the snow has given you an appetite, so how about something to eat?"

"Thank you," said Tasseltip. "I am a bit hungry."

Mr Mole went off to the kitchen to fetch some lettuce and chopped carrots for Tasseltip.

Soon Tasseltip was munching his way through the large snack Mr Mole put before him.

"Now," said Mr Mole, "I shall just go and see if my sister is on her way back."

"Thank you, Mr Mole," said Tasseltip, half rising to his feet as Mr Mole went out. Sitting down again, Tasseltip took a large mouthful of carrots.

Before long he heard voices, the door opened and there were the two Moles. Nurse Mole was wearing her uniform blue dress, with its starched white apron and frilly cap.

"Good morning, Tasseltip," said Nurse Mole. "I am sorry to hear your grandmother isn't feeling well. I shall be going out on my rounds very soon, so I will add her to my list of people to see."

Tasseltip finished his last mouthful and stood up. "Good morning," he said politely. "Granny will be very pleased if you can go to see her."

"You needn't come with me now, but perhaps you will call in and see her this afternoon, just in case there's anything she wants," said Nurse Mole.

Tasseltip promised he would, then he thanked Mr Mole and said goodbye. Next moment he was racing along the tunnel towards the back door.

Tasseltip opened Mr Mole's back door, and there he was out in the snow again. He could hear the noise of laughter and shouting as his friends rode down the slippery slope on the tray. He set off as quickly as he could to join them, waving his arms as he drew nearer.

Friskie whizzed past Tasseltip down the hill, shouting, "You can have the next turn. It's terrific fun."

"Come on, Tasseltip, we'd begun to give you up for lost. Where have you been?" said Robert, when his friend reached the top of the hill.

"Nurse Mole wasn't there, so I had to wait. You know how kind Mr Mole is. He thought I might be hungry and he gave me so much lettuce and carrot, I don't think I'll need anything else to eat today!" Tasseltip told him, watching Friskie struggling up the hill with the tray.

"I hope you saved some for us!" said Susie, jumping up and down to keep warm.

Friskie appeared at the top of the hill. "Your turn, Tasseltip. Come on, it's terrific fun."

Tasseltip climbed on, and held onto the piece of rope, then he nodded to Robert to push him off. Whoosh! He went flying down the hill, spraying snow all over the place as he went.

Tasseltip enjoyed it so much that when he got to the bottom, he couldn't imagine a better way to spend a snowy day.

Whilst Tasseltip was climbing up, Frankie and Susie began snowballing each other. Soon the air was filled with snow. Frankie Frog was winning, but just in time Susie noticed Tasseltip arriving with the tray. Quickly she leapt on it, and was just about to push off when Friskie saw what she was doing.

"Susie! Tasseltip is to have another turn," he shouted, and tried to pull her off. Instead the tray began slithering backwards down the steep hill, and soon they were both travelling at full speed towards the bottom.

At the top, Tasseltip, Frankie and Robert roared with laughter as they watched the brother and sister whizzing down the hill backwards!

"What are they holding onto?" asked Tasseltip. "When I went down, I held onto the rope pretty tightly in case I fell off."

"I think they will be all right," said Robert. "Friskie is holding onto Susie, so they can't come to much harm. Besides, the snow is very soft if they do fall off."

"Look, they've reached the bottom," said Tasseltip, gazing downwards. "Come on, let's go down to meet them."

"Oh! That was exciting!" said Susie.

"You weren't meant to have a turn then," said Friskie. "It should have been Tasseltip. I was trying to stop you, but it didn't quite work."

"I know, but I had to get away from Frankie Frog," said Susie. "He was winning our snowball fight."

"Come on, let's go and meet the others. It looks as if they are going to meet us half way," said Friskie, bending to pick up the string on the tray.

"You leave that alone!" shouted an angry-sounding voice. There was grumpy Mr Hedgehog. He was waving his fists in the air.

"Look, there's Mr Hedgehog," said Tasseltip suddenly. "I wonder what he's doing?"

"He seems to be saying something to Friskie and Susie," replied Frankie Frog. "I think he is angry with them, look how he is waving his fists in the air. I wonder what they can have been up to?"

"I think we ought to hurry down and find out," said Tasseltip. "You know what he's like when he's in a bad temper." So they set off down the hill.

Friskie and Susie sensibly left the tray alone and waited for Tasseltip and the others.

"So you are responsible, Tasseltip Rabbit," shouted Mr Hedgehog angrily. "I might have known!"

"Responsible? What do you mean, responsible?"

"This is what I mean, as you all very well know," said Mr Hedgehog, and he bent down and picked up the tray. "How dare you use this as a toboggan!" He started to walk off with the tray balanced on his head.

Tasseltip gazed after him in astonishment. Then, finding his voice, he shouted, "Mr Hedgehog, you can't take the tray away like that. It's ours. At least it's Robert's."

Mr Hedgehog stopped for a moment and turned around to look at Tasseltip. "You know perfectly well this is MY tray, you impertinent rascal." He glared round at all the friends, then turned and stomped off.

"What's he talking about, it's his tray?" said Tasseltip. "Robert, why didn't you tell him it's yours?"

But there was no sign of Robert.

"Where on earth has he got to?" asked Friskie.

"It's a mystery," said Tasseltip. "Well, as we can't play any more, I think I'm going home."

When Tasseltip reached home his mother was busy cooking. She looked up as she heard him open the door. "Is that you, Tasseltip? Where have you been? I thought I told you to come home first, before going out to play!"

"I'm very sorry," said Tasseltip. "But you see, I met Robert who had this tray, and he helped me to carry the basket to Granny's, and then after I had seen Nurse Mole . . ."

"Start at the beginning," said Mrs Rabbit. "I can make neither head nor tail of what you are saying at the moment."

So Tasseltip explained what had happened during the morning, and how Nurse Mole had asked him to go over to Granny's in the afternoon to see if he could do anything else.

"That's all right, then," said Mrs Rabbit sounding relieved. "I was a bit worried that Granny might be really ill when you didn't come home."

"Then a really strange thing happened," said Tasseltip. He went on to tell his mother all about Mr Hedgehog finding them playing, and taking the tray away, and how Robert Rat had suddenly disappeared without anyone noticing which way he went, and no one knew why.

"That certainly does sound a little odd," said Mrs Rabbit. "Mrs Rat is coming to tea with me this afternoon, so I will ask her what it's all about. If you go over to Granny's when you have finished eating, you can come back here in time to see her."

"Yes, I think I will do that," said Tasseltip.

Tasseltip set off once more towards his grandmother's little cottage.

Whistling happily as he walked along, he puzzled over Robert's disappearance and Mr Hedgehog's curious behaviour. "Never mind," he said to himself. "As long as Granny doesn't want too much done, I can easily be home in time to see Mrs Rat, and find out what's going on."

Just as he rounded a bend in the path, some snow fell in front of him. He looked right and left, but nothing moved. "Must be the snow falling off the branches of the trees," he thought. "I think the sun is causing some of it to melt."

All of a sudden he heard the bushes rustling, then he felt two arms around his neck and a heavy weight on his back. "Gee up," shouted Frankie, laughing and clinging on tightly. "You are my horse! Gee up!"

"It's jolly hard being a horse when it's all slippery like this. I can't breathe. Move your arms down a bit," said Tasseltip.

Then he set off at a tremendous speed, slipping and sliding along, with Frankie clinging on tightly.

Glancing over his shoulder as he ran, Tasseltip saw Friskie and Susie Squirrel behind him.

"Wait for us, Tasseltip," shouted Friskie.

"Sorry, can't stop. I'm a horse," he shouted back.

"That's enough now, Tasseltip," begged Frankie. "Thank you for a nice ride."

"I haven't finished yet," answered Tasseltip, seeing a hollow filled with snow just in front of him. Putting on an extra spurt he ran up to it, and tossed Frankie over his head into the pile of snow!

"Oooh! Help!" yelled Frankie as he sank into the deep snow, waving his legs in the air.

"What are you doing?" asked Friskie, coming up. "You do look funny."

"Did Tasseltip throw you into the snow?" asked Susie, as she reached the friends.

"Help me out," begged Frankie. "I can't get up."

"Serves you right," laughed Tasseltip. "I'll help you if you promise not to jump on me again."

"I promise, I promise," spluttered Frankie. "It's very cold sitting here."

"I'll help you," said Friskie, stretching out his hand. "Up you come."

"What are you going to do this afternoon?" Friskie asked Tasseltip.

"I'm going to see how my grandmother is and then I have to go home. Mrs Rat is coming to tea with my mother, so I thought I would be able to find out why Robert disappeared when Old Grumpy took the tray away."

"Good idea. Well, we're off to the woods," said Friskie. "Maybe we'll see you later on."

Tasseltip hopped and skipped along the path towards his grandmother's cottage, and peeped in through the window.

There, sitting side by side, warm and cosy by the fire, were his grandmother and Nurse Mole. They were both drinking large cups of steaming nettle tea. "Come on in, dear," called Granny.

"Hello," said Tasseltip. "Are you feeling better? I promised Nurse Mole I would look in and see if there was anything I could do."

"I'm feeling a lot better, thank you," said Granny.

"I want you to go to Dr Badger's to get a bottle of medicine for Granny," said Nurse Mole, handing Tasseltip a piece of paper. "Give this to him."

"Yes, all right," said Tasseltip, and off he went.

Tasseltip set off down the hill to Dr Badger's house. He wished he had a tray to use as a toboggan.

He passed quickly through the woods and was soon in sight of the Doctor's house. He went up to the front door and looked at the big brass plate with Dr Badger's name and the words *Please knock and wait* written on it.

So Tasseltip knocked loudly and waited.

Suddenly the door flew open and an angry-looking Dr Badger stood there. Poor Tasseltip was so startled that he lost his balance, and fell over backwards!

"Please, sir," stammered Tasseltip, very surprised by Dr Badger's angry manner, "I have a note from Nurse Mole. It's for some medicine for my grandmother. She has a very bad cold."

Dr Badger looked at Tasseltip for a minute, then said, "So it isn't you who keeps knocking on my door, and running off to hide when I open it?"

"No, sir," said a scared Tasseltip.

"Hmph," snorted the doctor, "must be some other young mischief maker. Let me see this note."

Dr Badger read it in silence.

RING

Dr Badger finished reading the note, and was just about to go into the house to make up the prescription, when a sudden gust of wind blew his hat off and into the tree above.

Dr Badger was very fond of his hat, and always wore it in the house. It was like a bright red pill box, with a nice yellow stripe around the edge, but what he particularly liked about this hat was the long tassel that hung down from it.

"Oh dear, oh dear," he said. "If it isn't bad enough having to put up with this dreadful cold weather, and now my hat has gone. Gone, just like that!"

"Please, sir, I could help you get it down," said Tasseltip. "If I can find a long enough stick, I can probably knock it down."

Tasseltip broke off a twig from a tree and reached up towards the hat. As he knocked it off the branch, a delighted Dr Badger caught it as it fell.

"Thank you for rescuing my hat," he said to Tasseltip. He went into the house, and was soon back carrying a medicine bottle which he handed to Tasseltip.

"Don't drop it!" he said.

"I won't. Thank you, Dr Badger," said Tasseltip.

Carrying the bottle of medicine, Tasseltip turned towards the path leading to his house. To his surprise he was suddenly bombarded by snowballs. Holding up his arm to protect his face,

Tasseltip tried to see who it was.

Then he heard a laugh. Susie Squirrel!

Tasseltip looked up, and there was Susie, well hidden in a fir tree. "I haven't got any more snowballs," she said, climbing down. "It was so funny to see Dr Badger so angry with you!"

"So it was you who kept knocking on his door and running away," said Tasseltip.

"He opened the door just as I was about to call and tell you what I had been doing. I'm sorry you had to take all the blame."

"That's all right," said Tasseltip, good-naturedly. "What are you doing here, all on your own? I thought you were with Friskie and Frankie Frog this afternoon, playing in the woods."

"We were," said Susie, a little gloomily. "Then Friskie decided they weren't going to play with girls, so I left them."

"Poor old you," laughed Tasseltip. "Look, I have to go home with this bottle of medicine. I'll come half way with you, and then you go and join Friskie and Frankie. Tell them I'll come and play as soon as I can."

So they walked along together until it was time to go their separate ways.

When Tasseltip opened the door, he found his mother talking to Mrs Rat. To his surprise, Robert was there too.

"Hello, everyone," said Tasseltip, coming into the room. "I've seen the doctor and he has given me a bottle of medicine for Granny. Do you want me to take it to her right away?"

"No, don't bother. I shall go and see her a little later on, so I will take it," said Mrs Rabbit, putting the bottle on the table.

"What happened, Robert?" asked Tasseltip. "When Mr Hedgehog appeared this morning, we looked around for you, but you'd vanished."

"Sorry, I didn't mean to cause any bother," said Robert. "I thought it best to go and sort the matter out with Mrs Hedgehog, and guess what — she has exactly the same tray as the one my mother gave me to use as a toboggan!"

"I never thought of that," said Tasseltip, laughing. "None of us could understand what it was all about."

"I've got it back, anyway," grinned Robert. "There's still some time left before it gets too dark, so let's go out to play again."

Tasseltip and Robert set off towards the hill, carrying the tray.

"I told Susie we would go and meet her. She was playing with Friskie and Frankie Frog, before she went off on her own. I persuaded her to go back, and told her we'd find them all together," Tasseltip told Robert.

"That sounds fine," said Robert. "I do think that all this snow is fun. I hope it lasts for ages."

"So do I," agreed Tasseltip, and the two of them ran along the path towing the tray toboggan.

"There are the Squirrels," said Robert.

"Hello, come and join us," shouted Tasseltip. "Robert has got the tray back."

"Hooray," shouted the Squirrels and Frankie.

In no time at all, they were taking it in turns to whoosh down the hill on the tray. Up and down, up and down they went. But trudging up the hill took longer and longer each time, until at last tiredness and darkness overtook them and they decided it must be time to go home.

"It was a super idea of yours," said Tasseltip to Robert, watching the Squirrels struggling up the hill for the last time. "We've had a lovely day."

"Haven't we!" agreed Robert. "A lovely day."

As they said goodbye and goodnight to each other, a few feather-like snowflakes began to fall. All the friends were so pleased. Tomorrow would be another lovely day, with lots of snow to play in.

The squirrels lived in these woods

Mr Mole: Tradesmen's entrance

This is the hill they whizzed down

The flower show was held in the Deep Wood

They gathered flowers here

WEASEL HOUSE

Mr Mole's house

They looked for the 'Boozle' here

Hedgehog's house

The Voles lived in this old stump